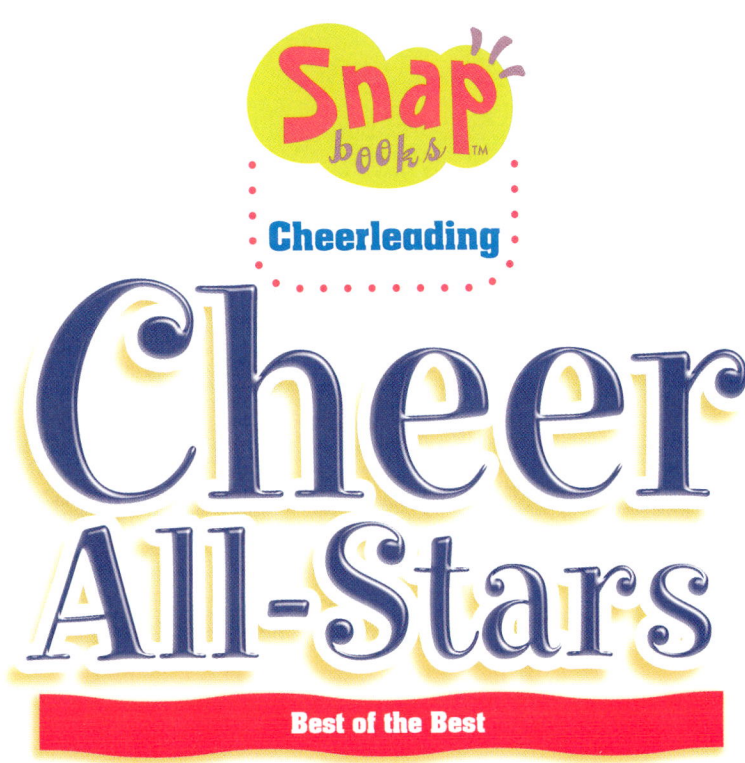

Cheerleading

Cheer All-Stars

Best of the Best

by Jen Jones

Content Consultant

Kristalynn Russell

Director and Choreographer,
Colorado Rapids Cheerleaders
Commerce City, Colorado

Capstone press®

Mankato, Minnesota

Snap Books are published by Capstone Press,
151 Good Counsel Drive, P.O. Box 669, Mankato, Minnesota 56002.
www.capstonepress.com

Cataloging-in-Publication data
Jones, Jen.
    Cheer all-stars: best of the best / by Jen Jones.
       p. cm. — (Snap books. Cheerleading)
Summary: "Upbeat text provides an in-depth look at all-star cheer squads and
describes their activities, opportunities, skills, and demands" — Provided by
publisher.
       Includes bibliographical references and index.
       ISBN-13: 978-1-4296-1346-0 (hardcover)
       ISBN-10: 1-4296-1346-7 (hardcover)
       1. Cheerleading — Competitions — Juvenile literature. 2. Cheerleading —
Juvenile literature. I. Title. II. Series.
LB3635.J618 2008
791.6'4 — dc22   2007018175

Editorial Credits

Jenny Marks, editor; Kim Brown, designer; Jo Miller, photo researcher

Photo Credits

Corbis/Kevin Dodge, 23
iStockphoto/Sean Locke, cover
Jamie Christian Photography, 5, 7, 8, 9, 12, 13 (both), 15, 16, 17, 19, 21, 25, 27, 28–29
Michele Torma Lee, 32
Phil Savage, 10–11

1 2 3 4 5 6 13 12 11 10 09 08

Table of Contents

Introduction 4

CHAPTER 1
Where Skill and Spirit Meet 6

CHAPTER 2
Let Your All-Star Light Shine 14

CHAPTER 3
Life in the Competition Lane 22

Glossary 30

Fast Facts 30

Read More 31

Internet Sites 31

About the Author 32

Index 32

Hey Now, You're an All-Star

Lace up your kicks and pack your poms. You're about to go on an amazing all-star journey!

All-star cheerleaders travel to new places and experience the thrills of competition. It's both glamorous and gritty. For every exciting performance, there are hours of practice. Luckily, the hard work doesn't go unnoticed. As all-star cheer explodes in growth, cheerleading continues to gain respect as a sport.

In this book, you'll find out what it takes to make it as an all-star. You'll learn the secrets of cheer success and meet the teams that have reached the top.

Chapter 1

WHERE SKILL AND SPIRIT MEET

All Cheer, All the Time

For more than 100 years, the role of cheerleaders was encouraging sports teams. All-star cheerleading has changed that tradition. Cheer gyms, not schools, create these squads. The best cheerleaders from many schools form dream teams that exist only to compete. All-star cheer transports cheerleaders from the sidelines to the spotlight!

Of course, all-star cheer isn't all or nothing. Many all-star cheerleaders cheer at school too. Some consider cheer double-duty to be the best of both worlds. These cheerleaders experience the excitement of all-star competition and the spirited rush of school games. However, doubling up can be stressful. Double-duty cheerleaders must master more routines and put in twice the time. Scheduling conflicts are bound to happen and require cooperation between coaches. Yet with hard work and dedication, these all-stars do it all.

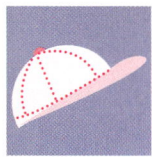

Kiddies and Coeds

Check out any cheer gym, and you'll find many squads under one roof. There are all-star divisions for cheerleaders of all ages. Each age group is divided into squads by skill level (1–5), team size, and all-girl or coed.

Whether you're a pint-sized powerhouse or a high school ham, you can be an all-star cheerleader. At tryouts, coaches decide what team you belong on. As you improve, you move up through the levels in your age group. Level 1 teams are for beginners. The experts compete in Level 5 squads.

The official competitive divisions include:

Tiny: 5 years and younger

Mini: 6 to 8 years

Youth: 9 to 11 years

Junior: 12 to 14 years

Senior: 16 to 18 years

Open: 18 years and older

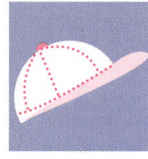

Gym Dandy

Want to get to the heart of the all-star action? Try out at a cheer gym! In recent times, the demand for all-star gyms has soared. In the late '90s, only about 200 gyms existed. Today, there are more than 2,500! The growth is especially noticeable in Texas and Florida. These two states have the most cheer gyms.

A typical cheer gym looks a lot like a gymnastics center. Safety mats and high ceilings make it easy to build tall stunts and flip the day away. Cheerleaders attend practice, take tumbling classes, and meet with coaches. Some gyms also offer cheer clinics and open-gym hours. At a cheer gym, practice makes perfect!

Pop Goes the All-Star Team

All-star squads aren't only found at cheer gyms. Pop Warner and other after-school clubs offer excellent all-star programs. One such program, Maximum Cheer All-Stars, is incredibly successful. Housed within the Boys' and Girls' Club in Lansdale, Pennsylvania, the program boasts more than 25 national champion titles!

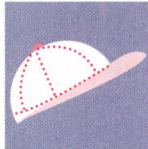

Something to Strive For

Baseball has the Yankees. Basketball has the Lakers. Football has the Patriots. Just like the rest of the sports world, all-star cheer has its own repeat champs. Certain programs seem to be magnets for national and world titles.

Cheer Athletics (Dallas, Texas)

In 1994, this program started in a park with two coaches and two cheerleaders. Today, Cheer Athletics has won four World Championships — more than any other all-star team.

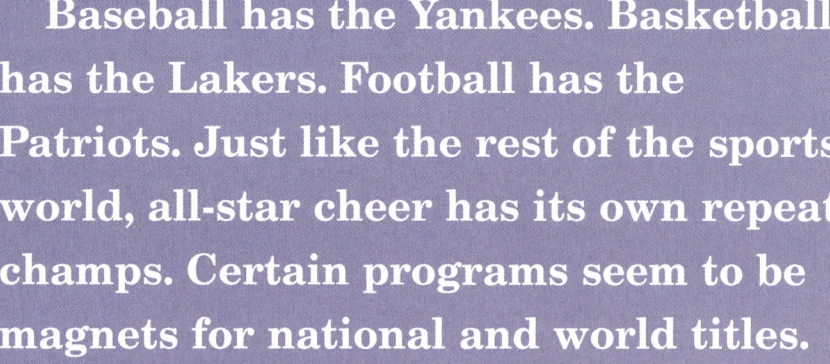

Gym Tyme (Louisville, Kentucky)

Southern states are known for fierce competition and cheer excellence. Right in the heart of "Cheer Country," Gym Tyme is a cheer machine! In 2006, the program brought home two gold medals from the World Championships.

Maryland Twisters (Glen Burnie, Maryland)

The Twisters are a force to be reckoned with! This spirited program has 11 teams. Altogether, they've landed more than 150 national titles and one world title.

Whatever It Takes

If cheerleaders got report cards, some of the subjects might be dance, tumbling, jumps, and spirit. And all-star athletes would be straight-A students! They stay in tip-top shape to make tough 3-minute routines look easy. From landing full twists to busting out show-stopping dance moves, all-star cheerleaders do it all!

14

Making the squad means stepping up your game. All-star teams attract the area's top cheerleaders. Being an all-star also means making sacrifices. Cheerleaders and their families devote many hours of hard work and hard-earned money. The demands are great, but the rewards are far greater.

BEST!

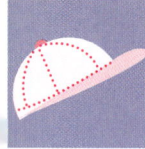

I'll Tumble for Ya

Tumbling is a big part of the all-star world. In fact, many squads have required tumbling skills. A Level 2 squad might call for a back handspring. Level 5 cheerleaders may have to master a full twist. High expectations don't end at tryouts. To nail tumbling moves in competition routines, all-stars train year-round.

Most routines feature two types of tumbling. In running tumbling, athletes take a running start to gain momentum. Then they complete a series of gymnastics moves, called a tumbling pass. In standing tumbling, cheerleaders flip from a standing position. Tumbling without a running start is difficult. It requires strength and control.

The "Ooh" Factor

Difficult tumbling tricks are real crowd-pleasers. Some fan favorites include standing back tucks, x-out flips, and full twisting layouts. Land one of these, and you're guaranteed to score points with the audience and the judges!

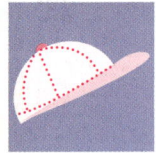

Stunt Girls

Liberties and cupies and scorpions, oh my! Top-level stunts take not only strength but teamwork and skill. To wow judges, stunts must be solid, difficult, and unique. Cheerleaders often move from one stunt into another. The results are stunning. A stunt series can make or break a routine.

In an all-star squad, cheerleaders divide into stunt teams. Each team has bases, spotters, and a flier. Each role is equally important. The bases lift and support the flier, while the flier shows off on top. Spotters watch the stunt for safety reasons. If the fliers and bases start to stumble, spotters lend helping hands. When stunting, there's no room for drama. Safe cooperation is the name of the game!

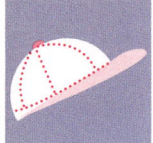

Let the Music Play

So what's the biggest difference between traditional cheerleading and all-star cheerleading? It's the lack of, well, cheers! All-star routines are all about entertainment. For that reason, the whole routine is set to music. There are no breaks for cheering. In order to beat the competition, a routine needs a killer beat!

Besides a fresh music mix, all-star routines must have dazzling choreography. Flashy dance moves add a visual layer to stunts and pile on the excitement. Many routines feature a dance portion performed by the entire squad. Crowd-pleasing moves and showmanship are a must! Add a dose of fancy footwork, and your squad is one step closer to a trophy.

On the Road Again

It's the weekend. Time to relax, right? Not if you're on an all-star squad. Some squads travel to cheer competitions every weekend. Being on the go is part of all-star life. Some teams spend almost as much time on the road as they do cheering. If you are a jet-setting all-star, check out these travel tips.

So you're stuck on the bus? Make the most of it! Play some team-building games or sing silly songs. Celeb or style magazines also help pass the time.

Use travel time to reflect on your competition goals. Clearly imagining a win makes it more likely to happen.

National competitions are often held in sunny locations like Florida or Las Vegas. Take advantage of rare downtime by going sightseeing or taking a dip in the pool!

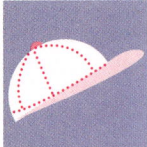

Pack on the Points

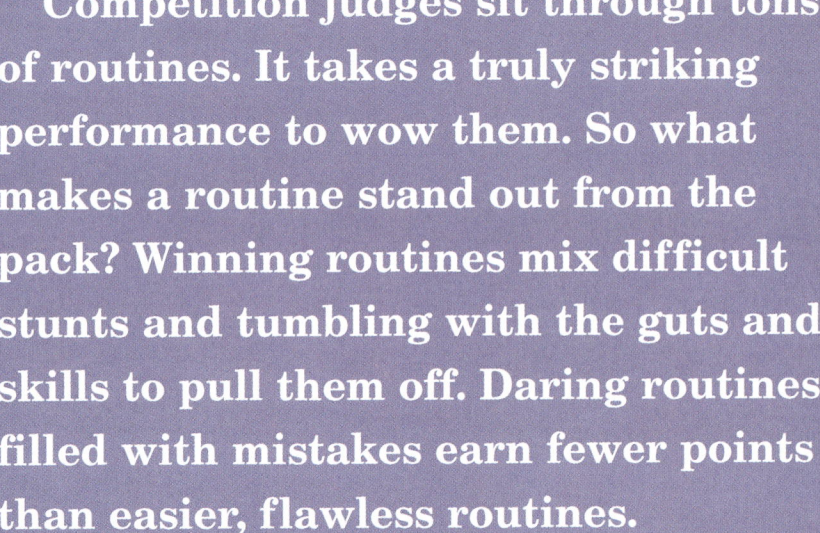

Competition judges sit through tons of routines. It takes a truly striking performance to wow them. So what makes a routine stand out from the pack? Winning routines mix difficult stunts and tumbling with the guts and skills to pull them off. Daring routines filled with mistakes earn fewer points than easier, flawless routines.

Want an easy way to boost your team's points? Play by the rules. Even the best squad loses points by breaking them. Attention to all the little details can pay off big in the end.

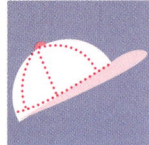

The Path to Nationals

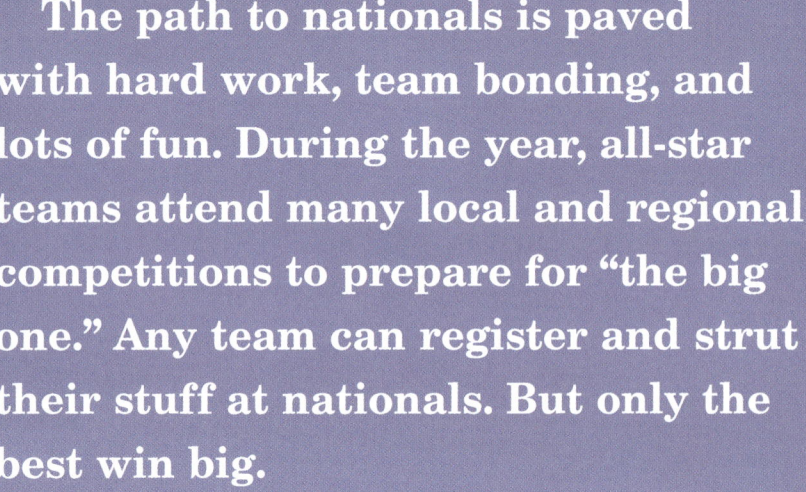

The path to nationals is paved with hard work, team bonding, and lots of fun. During the year, all-star teams attend many local and regional competitions to prepare for "the big one." Any team can register and strut their stuff at nationals. But only the best win big.

Some of the most well-known national competitions include:

UCA National All-Star Cheerleading Championship

The NASCC is held every March in Orlando, Florida. This competition draws top all-star teams from across the country. Bonus: the event is shown on ESPN.

NCA All-Star National Championship

The NASNC is held in a sweet spot for all-star cheerleading — Texas! The competition attracts talented local teams like Cheer Athletics and Spirit of Texas.

USASF Cheerleading Worlds

The Worlds competition is like the Olympics of all-star cheer. When a team rocks a national competition, they may be awarded a bid to attend Worlds. The winners are simply the best!

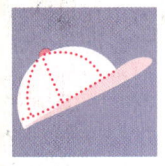

The Real Rewards

All-star cheerleaders live the cheer life 24/7. They focus their bodies and minds on intense preparation. Working so hard to win can make it heartbreaking if it doesn't happen. But all-star cheer is about much more than snagging first place. Although winning is great proof of a team's dedication, the real rewards come from the experience.

The benefits of cheer extend far beyond the competition floor. Laughter shared over silly practice moments can lead to lifelong friendships. The leadership skills formed on the squad shine through at work and school. Improved confidence, fitness, and health are just a few other all-star perks. All-stars truly become stars — on and off the floor!